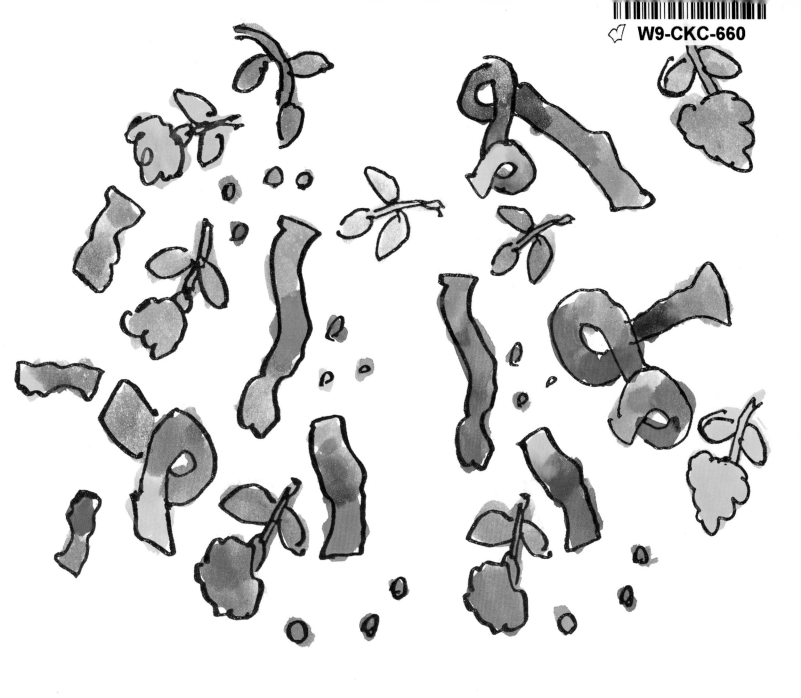

For A.M.B.

PARADE
A Bantam Little Rooster Book/August 1990

Little Rooster is a trademark of Bantam Books,
a division of Bantam Doubleday Dell Publishing Group, Inc.

Library of Congress Cataloging-in-Publication Data
Ziefert, Harriet.
Parade/by Harriet Ziefert; illustrated by Saul Mandel.
p. cm.
"A Bantam little rooster book."
Summary: Highlights the tastes and smells, the sounds and sights of the circus parade.
ISBN 0-553-05862-2
[1. Parades—Fiction. 2. Circus—Fiction. 3. Stories in rhyme.]
I. Mandel, Saul, ill. II. Title. PZ8.3.Z49Par 1990 [E]—dc20

89-17549
CIP
AC

Published simultaneously in the United States and Canada

Bantam Books are published by Bantam Books, a division of Bantam Doubleday Dell
Publishing Group, Inc. Its trademark, consisting of the words "Bantam Books" and the
portrayal of a rooster, is Registered in U.S. Patent and Trademark Office and in other
countries. Marca Registrada, Bantam Books, 666 Fifth Avenue, New York, NY 10103.

PRINTED IN SINGAPORE FOR HARRIET ZIEFERT, INC.

0 9 8 7 6 5 4 3 2 1

Parade

By Harriet Ziefert

Illustrated by Saul Mandel

A BANTAM LITTLE ROOSTER BOOK
NEW YORK · TORONTO · LONDON · SYDNEY · AUCKLAND

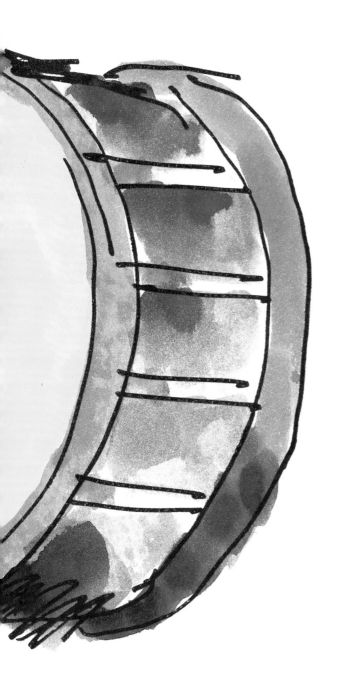

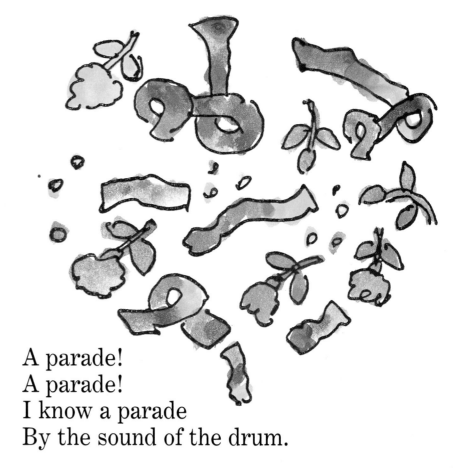

A parade!
A parade!
I know a parade
By the sound of the drum.

A-rum-a-tee-tum!
A-rum-a-tee-tum!

Here it comes
Down the street.

I know a parade
By the sound
Of the feet.

Music and feet.
Music and feet.

Can't you feel
The sound
And the beat?

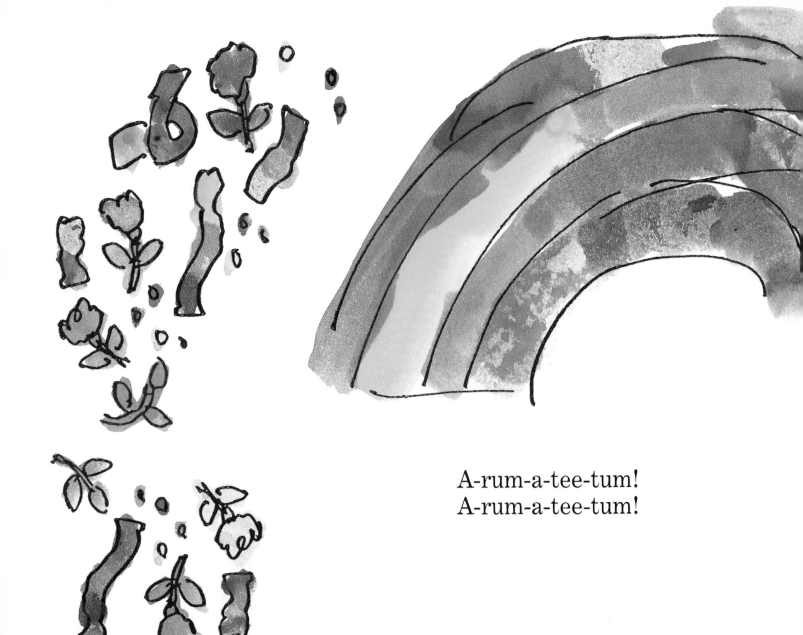

A-rum-a-tee-tum!
A-rum-a-tee-tum!

Here comes a clown
Down the street.

I know a clown
By the nose and the feet.

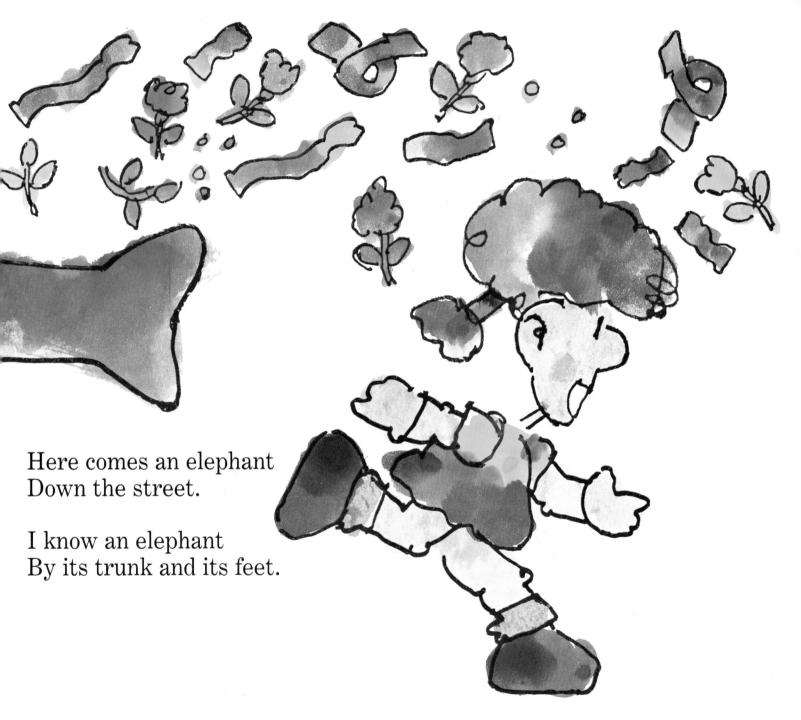

Here comes an elephant
Down the street.

I know an elephant
By its trunk and its feet.

Here come horses down the street.
Music and feet. Music and feet.

Can't you feel the sound and the beat?
A-rum-a-tee-tum! A-rum-a-tee-tum!

A-rum-a-tee
Rum-a-tee
Rum-a-tee-tum!

Now jugglers…now acrobats…

now strong men…now twirlers!

Taste the candy.

Smell the popcorn.

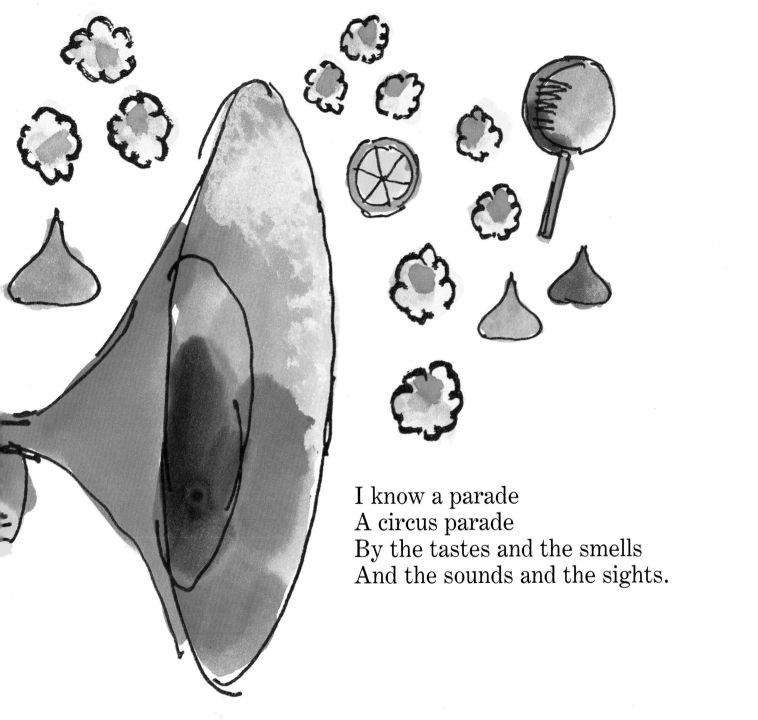

I know a parade
A circus parade
By the tastes and the smells
And the sounds and the sights.

Here we come
Down the street.

A-rum-a-tee-tum!
A-rum-a-tee-tum!

A-rum-a-tee
Rum-a-tee
Rum-a-tee-tum!